Bemerkungen über Frazers *Golden Bough*
Remarks on Frazer's *Golden Bough*

Bemerkungen über Frazers

GOLDEN BOUGH

Ludwig Wittgenstein

herausgegeben von RUSH RHEES

HUMANITIES PRESS, INC.
Atlantic Highlands, New Jersey

Remarks on Frazer's

GOLDEN BOUGH

Ludwig Wittgenstein

edited by RUSH RHEES

English translation by A.C. Miles   **revised by** Rush Rhees

HUMANITIES PRESS, INC.
Atlantic Highlands, New Jersey

First Published in the United States of America
in 1979
By Humanities Press Inc.
Atlantic Highlands, N.J. 07716
Printed in Great Britain

Copyright © The Brynmill Press Ltd

Library of Congress Cataloguing in Publication Data

Wittgenstein, Ludwig, 1889–1951.
  Remarks on Frazer's Golden bough

  Translation of Bemerkungen über Frazers Golden
bough.
  1. Frazer, James George, Sir, 1854–1941. The
golden bough. 2. Mythology. 3. Religion, Primitive.
4. Magic. 5. Superstition.
I. Rhees, Rush. II. Title.
BL310.F73W5713   291   79-4038
ISBN 0-391-00984-2

Dr. M. O'C. Drury writes: "I think it would have been in 1930 that Wittgenstein said to me that he had always wanted to read Frazer but hadn't done so, and would I get hold of a copy and read some of it out loud to him. I borrowed from the Union Library the first volume of the multi-volume edition and we only got a little way through this because he talked at considerable length about it, and the next term we didn't start it again." – Wittgenstein began writing on Frazer in his manuscript book on June 19th, 1931, and he added remarks during the next two or three weeks – although he was writing more about other things (such as Verstehen eines Satzes, Bedeutung, Komplex und Tatsache, Intention...). He may have made earlier notes in a pocket notebook, but I have found none.

It was probably in 1931 that he dictated to a typist the greater part of the manuscript books written since July 1930; often changing the order of remarks, and details of the phrasing, but leaving large blocks as they stood. (He rearranged the material again and again later on.) This particular typescript runs to 771 pages. It has a section, just under 10 pages long, of the remarks on Frazer, with a few changes in order and phrasing. Others are in different contexts, and a few are left out.

The typed section on Frazer begins with three remarks which are not connected with them in the manuscript. He had begun there with remarks which he later marked S (='schlecht') and did not have typed. I think we can see why. The earlier version was:

"Ich glaube jetzt, daß es richtig wäre, mein Buch mit Bemerkungen über die Metaphysik als eine Art von Magie zu beginnen.

Worin ich aber weder der Magie das Wort reden noch mich über sie lustig machen darf.

Von der Magie müßte die Tiefe behalten werden. –

Ja, das Ausschalten der Magie hat hier den Charakter der Magie selbst.

Denn, wenn ich damals anfing von der '*Welt*' zu reden (und nicht von diesem Baum oder Tisch), was wollte ich anderes als ctwas Höheres in meine Worte bannen." *

He wrote the second set of remarks – and they are only rough notes – years later; not earlier than 1936 and probably after 1948. They are written in pencil on odd bits of paper; probably he meant to insert the smaller ones in the copy of the one-volume edition of *The Golden Bough* that he was using. Miss Anscombe found them among some of his things after his death.

RUSH RHEES

* "I think now that the right thing would be to begin my book with re-marks about metaphysics as a kind of magic.

But in doing this I must neither speak in defence of magic nor ridicule it.

What it is that is deep about magic would be kept. ——

In this context, in fact, keeping magic out has itself the character of magic.

For when I began in my earlier book to talk about the '*world*' (and not about this tree or table), was I trying to do anything except conjure up some-thing of a higher order by my words?"

I

Man muß beim Irrtum ansetzen und **ihn in** die Wahrheit überführen.

D.h., man muß die Quelle des Irrtums aufdecken, sonst nützt uns das Hören der Wahrheit nichts. Sie kann nicht eindringen, wenn etwas anderes ihren Platz einnimmt.

Einen von der Wahrheit zu überzeugen, genügt es nicht, die Wahrheit zu konstatieren, sondern man muß den *Weg* von Irrtum zur Wahrheit finden.

Ich muß immer wieder im Wasser des Zweifels untertauchen.

Frazers Darstellung der magischen und religiösen Anschauungen der Menschen ist unbefriedigend: sie läßt diese Anschauungen als *Irrtümer* erscheinen.

So war also Augustinus im Irrtum, wenn er Gott auf jeder Seite der *Confessionen* anruft?

Aber – kann man sagen – wenn er nicht im Irrtum war, so war es doch der Buddhistische Heilige – oder welcher immer – dessen Religion ganz andere Anschauungen zum Ausdruck bringt. Aber *keiner* von ihnen war im Irrtum, außer wo er eine Theorie aufstellte.

Schon die Idee, den Gebrauch – etwa die Tötung des Priesterkönigs – erklären zu wollen, scheint mir verfehlt. Alles was Frazer tut ist, sie Menschen, die so ähnlich denken wie er, plausibel zu machen. Es ist sehr merkwürdig, daß alle diese Gebräuche endlich so zu sagen als Dummheiten dargestellt werden.

Nie wird es aber plausibel, daß die Menschen aus purer Dummheit all das tun.

Wenn er uns z.B. erklärt, der König müsse in seiner Blüte getötet werden,

We must begin with the mistake and transform it into what is true.

That is, we must uncover the source of the error ; otherwise hearing what is true won't help us. It cannot penetrate when something is taking its place.

To convince someone of what is true, it is not enough to state it ; we must find the *road* from error to truth.

I must plunge again and again in the water of doubt.

Frazer's account of the magical and religious notions of men is unsatisfactory: it makes these notions appear as *mistakes*.

Was Augustine mistaken, then, when he called on God on every page of the *Confessions* ?

Well—one might say—if he was not mistaken, then the Buddhist holyman, or some other, whose religion expresses quite different notions, surely was. But *none* of them was making a mistake except where he was putting forward a theory.

Even the idea of trying to explain the practice—say the killing of the priest-king—seems to me wrong-headed. All that Frazer does is to make this practice plausible to people who think as he does. It is very queer that all these practices are finally presented, so to speak, as stupid actions.

But it never does become plausible that people do all this out of sheer stupidity.

When he explains to us, for example, that the king must be killed in

weil nach den Anschauungen der Wilden sonst seine Seele nicht frisch erhalten würde, so kann man doch nur sagen: wo jener Gebrauch und diese Anschauungen zusammengehn, dort entspringt nicht der Gebrauch der Anschauung, sondern sie sind eben beide da.

Es kann schon sein, und kommt heute oft vor, daß ein Mensch einen Gebrauch aufgibt, nachdem er einen Irrtum erkannt hat, auf den sich dieser Gebrauch stützte. Aber dieser Fall besteht eben nur dort, wo es genügt den Menschen auf seinen Irrtum aufmerksam zu machen, um ihn von seiner Handlungsweise abzubringen. Aber das ist doch bei den religiösen Gebräuchen eines Volkes nicht der Fall und *darum* handelt es sich eben um *keinen* Irrtum. *

Frazer sagt, es sei sehr schwer, den Irrtum in der Magie zu entdecken – und darum halte sie sich so lange – weil z.B. eine Beschwörung, die Regen herbeiführen soll, früher oder später gewiß als wirksam erscheint.†
Aber dann ist es eben merkwürdig, daß die Menschen nicht früher daraufkommen, daß es ohnehin früher oder später regnet.

Ich glaube, daß das Unternehmen einer Erklärung schon darum verfehlt ist, weil man nur richtig zusammenstellen muß, was man *weiß*, und nichts dazusetzen, und die Befriedigung, die durch die Erklärung angestrebt wird, ergibt sich von selbst.

Und die Erklärung ist es hier gar nicht, die befriedigt. Wenn Frazer anfängt und uns die Geschichte von dem Waldkönig von Nemi erzählt,

---

* Cf. *The Golden Bough*, page 264: " But reflection and enquiry should satisfy us that to our predecessors we are indebted for much of what we thought most our own, and that their errors were not wilful extravagances or the ravings of insanity, but simply hypotheses, justifiable as such at the time when they were propounded, but which a fuller experience has proved to be inadequate. It is only by the successive testing of hypotheses and rejection of the false that truth is at last elicited. After all, what we call truth is only the hypothesis which is found to work best. Therefore in reviewing the opinions and practices of ruder ages and races we shall do well to look with

his prime because, according to the notions of the savages, his soul would not be kept fresh otherwise, we can only say: where that practice and these views go together, the practice does not spring from the view, but both of them are there.

It may happen, as it often does today, that someone will give up a practice when he has seen that something on which it depended is an error.   But this happens only in cases where you can make a man change his way of doing things simply by calling his attention to his error.   This is not how it is in connexion with the religious practices of a people ; and what we have here is *not* an error.*

Frazer says it is very difficult to discover the error in magic and this is why it persists for so long—because, for example, a ceremony which is supposed to bring rain is sure to appear effective sooner or later.†

But then it is queer that people do not notice sooner that it does rain sooner or later anyway.

I think one reason why the attempt to find an explanation is wrong is that we have only to put together in the right way what we *know*, without adding anything, and the satisfaction we are trying to get from the the explanation comes of itself.

And here the explanation is not what satisfies us anyway.   When Frazer begins by telling the story of the King of the Wood at Nemi, he

leniency upon their errors as inevitable slips made in the search for truth, and to give them the benefit of that indulgence which we ourselves may one day stand in need of: *cum excusatione itaque veteres audiendi sunt.*"

† Cf. page 59: "A ceremony intended to make the wind blow or the rain fall, or to work the death of an enemy, will always be followed, sooner or later, by the occurrence it is meant to bring to pass; and primitive man may be excused for regarding the occurrence as a direct result of the ceremony, and the best possible proof of its efficacy."

so tut er dies in einem Ton, der zeigt, daß hier etwas Merkwürdiges und Furchtbares geschieht. Die Frage aber "warum geschieht dies?" wird eigentlich dadurch beantwortet: Weil es furchtbar ist. Das heißt, dasselbe, was uns bei diesem Vorgang furchtbar, großartig, schaurig, tragisch, etc., nichts weniger als trivial und bedeutungslos vorkommt, *das* hat diesen Vorgang ins Leben gerufen.

Nur *beschreiben* kann man hier und sagen: so ist das menschliche Leben.

Die Erklärung ist im Vergleich mit dem Eindruck, den uns das Beschriebene macht, zu unsicher.

Jede Erklärung ist eine Hypothese.

Wer aber, etwa, von der Liebe beunruhigt ist, dem wird eine hypothetische Erklärung wenig helfen. – Sie wird ihn nicht beruhigen.

Das Gedränge der Gedanken, die nicht herauskommen, weil sich alle vordrängen wollen und so am Ausgang verkeilen.

Wenn man mit jener Erzählung vom Priesterkönig von Nemi das Wort "die Majestät des Todes" zusammenstellt, so sieht man, daß die beiden Eins sind.
Das Leben des Priesterkönigs stellt das dar, was mit jenem Wort gemeint ist.

Wer von der Majestät des Todes ergriffen ist, kann dies durch so ein Leben zum Ausdruck bringen. – Dies ist natürlich auch keine Erklärung, sondern setzt nur ein Symbol für ein anderes. Oder: eine Zeremonie für eine andere.

Einem religiösen Symbol liegt keine *Meinung* zu Grunde.
Und nur der Meinung entspricht der Irrtum.

Man möchte sagen: Dieser und dieser Vorgang hat stattgefunden; lach', wenn Du kannst.

does this in a tone which shows that something strange and terrible is happening here.   And that is the answer to the question " why is this happening ? " : Because it is terrible.   In other words, what strikes us in this course of events as terrible, impressive, horrible, tragic, &c., anything but trivial and insignificant, *that* is what gave birth to them.

We can only *describe* and say, human life is like that.

Compared with the impression that what is described here makes on us, the explanation is too uncertain.

Every explanation is an hypothesis.

But for someone broken up by love an explanatory hypothesis won't help much. — It will not bring peace.

The crush of thoughts that do not get out because they all try to push forward and are wedged in the door.

Put that account of the King of the Wood at Nemi together with the phrase " the majesty of death ", and you see that they are one.
The life of the priest-king shows what is meant by that phrase.

If someone is gripped by the majesty of death, then through such a life he can give expression to it. — Of course this is not an explanation : it puts one symbol in place of another.   Or one ceremony in place of another.

A religious symbol does not rest on any *opinion*.
And error belongs only with opinion.

One would like to say: This is what took place here; laugh, if you can.

Die religiöse Handlungen, oder das religiöse Leben des Priesterkönigs ist von keiner andern Art, als jede echt religiöse Handlung heute, etwa ein Geständnis der Sünden. Auch dieses läßt sich 'erklären' und läßt sich nicht erklären.

In Effigie verbrennen. Das Bild des Geliebten küssen. Das basiert *natürlich nicht* auf einem Glauben an eine bestimmte Wirkung auf den Gegenstand, den das Bild darstellt. Es bezweckt eine Befriedigung und erreicht sie auch. Oder vielmehr, es *bezweckt* gar nichts; wir handeln so und fühlen uns dann befriedigt.

Man könnte auch den Namen der Geliebten küssen, und hier wäre die Stellvertretung durch den Namen klar.

Der selbe Wilde, der, anscheinend um seinen Feind zu töten, dessen Bild durchsticht, baut seine Hütte aus Holz wirklich und schnitzt seinen Pfeil kunstgerecht und nicht in Effigie.

Die Idee, daß man einen leblosen Gegenstand zu sich herwinken kann, wie man einen Menschen zu sich herwinkt. Hier ist das Prinzip das, der Personifikation.

Und immer beruht die Magie auf der Idee des Symbolismus und der Sprache.

Die Darstellung eines Wunsches ist, eo ipso, die Darstellung seiner Erfüllung.
Die Magie aber bringt einen Wunsch zur Darstellung; sie äußert einen Wunsch.

Die Taufe als Waschung. – Ein Irrtum entsteht erst, wenn die Magie wissenschaftlich ausgelegt wird.
Wenn die Adoption eines Kindes so vor sich geht, daß die Mutter es durch ihre Kleider zieht, so ist es doch verrückt zu glauben, daß hier ein *Irrtum* vorliegt und sie glaubt, das Kind geboren zu haben.*

* "The same principle of make-believe, so dear to children, has led other

The religious actions or the religious life of the priest-king are not different in kind from any genuinely religious action today, say a confession of sins.   This also can be " explained " (made clear) and cannot be explained.

Burning in effigy.   Kissing the picture of a loved one.   This is obviously *not* based on a belief that it will have a definite effect on the object which the picture represents.   It aims at some satisfaction and it achieves it.   Or rather, it does not *aim* at anything; we act in this way and then feel satisfied.

One could also kiss the name of the loved one, and here the representation by the name would be clear.

The same savage who, apparently in order to kill his enemy, sticks his knife through a picture of him, really does build his hut of wood and cuts his arrow with skill and not in effigy.

The idea that one can beckon a lifeless object to come, just as one would beckon a person.   Here the principle is that of personification.

And magic always rests on the idea of symbolism and of language.

The description [*Darstellung*] of a wish is, *eo ipso*, the description of its fulfilment.
And magic does give representation [*Darstellung*] to a wish ; it expresses a wish.

Baptism as washing. — There is a mistake only if magic is presented as science.
If the adoption of a child is carried out by the mother pulling the child from beneath her clothes, then it is crazy to think there is an *error* in this and that she believes she has borne the child.*

---

peoples to employ a simulation of birth as a form of adoption. ... A woman will take a boy whom she intends to adopt and push or pull him through her clothes ; ever afterwards he is regarded as her very son, and inherits the whole property of his adoptive parents." (*The Golden Bough*, pp. 14, 15)

Von den magischen Operationen sind die zu unterscheiden, die auf einer falschen, zu einfachen, Vorstellung der Dinge und Vorgänge beruhen. Wenn man etwa sagt, die Krankheit ziehe von einem Teil des Körpers in den andern, oder Vorkehrungen trifft, die Krankheit abzuleiten, als wäre sie eine Flüssigkeit oder ein Wärmezustand. Man macht sich dann also ein falsches, das heißt hier, unzutreffendes Bild.

Welche Enge des seelischen Lebens bei Frazer! Daher: Welche Unmöglichkeit, ein anderes Leben zu begreifen, als das englische seiner Zeit!

Frazer kann sich keinen Priester vorstellen, der nicht im Grunde ein englischer Parson unserer Zeit ist, mit seiner ganzen Dummheit und Flauheit.

Warum sollte dem Menschen sein Name nicht heilig sein können. Ist er doch einerseits das wichtigste Instrument, das ihm gegeben wird, anderseits wie ein Schmuckstück, das ihm bei der Geburt umgehangen wird.

Wie irreführend die Erklärungen Frazers sind, sieht man – glaube ich – daraus, daß man primitive Gebräuche sehr wohl selbst erdichten könnte und es müßte ein Zufall sein, wenn sie nicht irgendwo wirklich gefunden würden. Das heißt, das Prinzip, nach welchem diese Gebräuche geordnet sind, ist ein viel allgemeineres als Frazer es erklärt und in unserer eigenen Seele vorhanden, so daß wir uns alle Möglichkeiten selbst ausdenken könnten. – Daß etwa der König eines Stammes für niemanden sichtbar wird, können wir uns wohl vorstellen, aber auch, daß jeder Mann des Stammes ihn sehen soll. Das letztere wird dann gewiß nicht in irgendeiner mehr oder weniger zufälligen Weise geschehen dürfen, sondern er wird den Leuten *gezeigt* werden. Vielleicht wird ihn niemand berühren dürfen, vielleicht aber berühren *müssen*. Denken wir daran, daß nach Schuberts Tod sein Bruder Partituren Schuberts in kleine Stücke zerschnitt und seinen Lieblingsschülern solche Stücke von einigen Takten gab. Diese Handlung, als Zeichen der Pietät, ist uns *ebenso* verständlich, wie die andere, die Partituren unberührt, niemandem zugänglich, aufzubewahren. Und hätte Schuberts Bruder die Partituren verbrannt, so wäre auch das als Zeichen der Pietät verständlich.

Das Zeremonielle (heiße oder kalte) im Gegensatz zum Zufälligen (lauen) charakterisiert die Pietät.

We should distinguish between magical operations and those operations which rest on a false, over-simplified notion of things and processes. For instance, if someone says that the illness is moving from one part of the body into another, or if he takes measures to draw off the illness as though it were a liquid or a temperature. He is then using a false picture, a picture that doesn't fit.

What narrowness of spiritual life we find in Frazer ! And as a result: how impossible for him to understand a different way of life from the English one of his time !

Frazer cannot imagine a priest who is not basically an English parson of our times with all his stupidity and feebleness.

Why should it not be possible that a man's own name be sacred to him ? Surely it is both the most important instrument given to him and also something like a piece of jewelry hung round his neck at birth.

Just how misleading Frazer's accounts are, we see, I think, from the fact that one could well imagine primitive practices oneself and it would only be by chance if they were not actually to be found somewhere. That is, the principle according to which these practices are ordered* is much more general than Frazer shows it to be and we find it in ourselves : we could think out for ourselves the different possibilities. — We can readily imagine that, say, in a given tribe no-one is allowed to see the king, or again that every man in the tribe is obliged to see him. And then it will certainly not be left more or less to chance, but the king will be *shown* to the people. Perhaps no-one will be allowed to touch him, or perhaps they will be *compelled* to do so. Think how after Schubert's death his brother cut certain of Schubert's scores into small pieces and gave to his favourite pupils these pieces of a few bars each. As a sign of piety this action is *just* as comprehensible to us as the other one of keeping the scores undisturbed and accessible to no-one. And if Schubert's brother had burnt the scores we could still understand this as a sign of piety.

The ceremonial (hot or cold) as opposed to the haphazard (lukewarm) is a characteristic of piety.

* I.e., how they stand related to one another and what this depends on.

Ja, Frazers Erklärungen wären überhaupt keine Erklärungen, wenn sie nicht letzten Endes an eine Neigung in uns selbst appellierten.

Das Essen und Trinken ist mit Gefahren verbunden, nicht nur für den Wilden, sondern auch für uns; nichts natürlicher, als daß man sich vor diesen schützen will; und nun könnten wir uns selbst solche Schutzmaßnahmen ausdenken. – Aber nach welchem Prinzip erdichten wir sie? Offenbar danach, daß alle Gefahren der Form nach auf einige sehr einfache reduziert werden, die dem Menschen ohne weiteres sichtbar sind. Also nach dem selben Prinzip, nach dem die ungebildete Leute unter uns sagen, die Krankheit ziehe sich vom Kopf in die Brust etc., etc.

In diesen einfachen Bildern wird natürlich die Personifikation eine große Rolle spielen, denn, daß Menschen (also Geister) dem Menschen gefärlich werden können, ist jedem bekannt.

Daß der Schatten des Menschen, der wie ein Mensch ausschaut, oder sein Spiegelbild, daß Regen, Gewitter, die Mondphasen, der Jahreszeitwechsel, die Ähnlichkeit und Verschiedenheit der Tiere unter einander und zum Menschen, die Erscheinungen des Todes, der Geburt und des Geschlechtslebens, kurz alles, was der Mensch jahraus jahrein um sich wahrnimmt, in mannigfaltigster Weise mit einander verknüpft, in seinem Denken (seiner Philosophie) und seinen Gebräuchen eine Rolle spielen wird, ist selbstverständlich, oder ist eben das, was wir wirklich wissen und interessant ist. *

Wie hätte das Feuer oder die Ähnlichkeit des Feuers mit der Sonne verfehlen können auf den erwachenden Menschengeist einen Eindruck zu machen. Aber nicht vielleicht "weil er sich's nicht erklären kann" (der dumme Aberglaube unserer Zeit) – denn wird es durch eine 'Erklärung' weniger eindrucksvoll? –

Die Magie in "Alice in Wonderland" beim Trocknen durch Vorlesen des Trockensten was es gibt. †

Bei der magischen Heilung einer Krankheit *bedeutet* man ihr, sie möge den Patienten verlassen.

---

* Auf einer spateren Stelle desselben Manuskriptbuchs steht: "Die eigentlichen Grundlagen seiner Forschung fallen dem Menschen gar nicht auf. Es sei denn, daß ihm *dies* einmal zum Bewußtsein gekommen ist. (Frazer etc., etc.)"

And Frazer's explanations would be no explanations at all if finally they did not appeal to an inclination in ourselves.

Eating and drinking have their dangers, not only for savages but also for us; nothing more natural than wanting to protect oneself against these; and we could think out protective measures ourselves. — But what principle do we follow in imagining them ? Clearly that of reducing the various forms of danger to a few very simple ones that anyone can see. In other words, the same principle that leads uneducated people in our society to say that the illness is moving from the head into the chest &c., &c. In these simple images personification will of course play a large part, for men (spirits) can become dangerous to a man and everyone knows this.

That a man's shadow, which looks like a man, or that his mirror image, or that rain, thunderstorms, the phases of the moon, the change of seasons, the likenesses and differences of animals to one another and to human beings, the phenomena of death, of birth and of sexual life, in short everything a man perceives year in, year out around him, connected together in any variety of ways—that all this should play a part in his thinking (his philosophy) and his practices, is obvious, or in other words this is what we really know and find interesting.*

How could fire or fire's resemblance to the sun have failed to make an impression on the awakening mind of man ? But not " because he can't explain it " (the stupid superstition of our time)—for does an " explanation " make it less impressive ?

The magic in *Alice in Wonderland,* trying to dry out by reading the driest thing there is. †

In magical healing one *indicates* to an illness that it should leave the patient.

* In another part of the same MS book Wittgenstein wrote: "It never occurs to a man what the foundations are on which his investigation really rests— unless perhaps *this* has occurred to him. (Frazer &c., &c.)"

† Chapter III, the remark of the mouse.

Man möchte nach der Beschreibung so einer magischen Kur immer sagen: Wenn *das* die Krankheit nicht versteht, so weiß ich nicht, *wie* man es ihr sagen soll.

Ich meine nicht, daß gerade das *Feuer* jedem einen Eindruck machen muß. Das Feuer nicht mehr, wie jede andere Erscheinung, und die eine Erscheinung Dem, die andere Jenem. Denn keine Erscheinung ist an sich besonders geheimnisvoll, aber jede kann es uns werden, und das ist eben das Charakteristische am erwachenden Geist des Menschen, daß ihm eine Erscheinung bedeutend wird. Man könnte fast sagen, der Mensch sei ein zeremonielles Tier. Das ist wohl teils falsch, teils unsinnig, aber es ist auch etwas Richtiges daran.

Das heißt, man könnte ein Buch über Anthropologie so anfangen: Wenn man das Leben und Benehmen der Menschen auf der Erde betrachtet, so sieht man, daß sie außer den Handlungen, die man tierische nennen könnte, der Nahrungsaufnahme, etc., etc., etc., auch solche ausführen, die einen eigentümlichen Charakter tragen und die man rituelle Handlungen nennen könnte.

Nun aber ist es Unsinn, so fortzufahren, daß man als das Charakteristische *dieser* Handlungen sagt, sie seien solche, die aus fehlerhaften Anschauungen über die Physik der Dinge entsprängen. (So tut es Frazer, wenn er sagt, Magie sei wesentlich falsche Physik, bzw. falsche Heilkunst, Technik, etc.)

Vielmehr ist das Charakteristische der rituellen Handlung gar keine Ansicht, Meinung, ob sie nun richtig oder falsch ist, obgleich eine Meinung – ein Glaube – selbst auch rituell sein kann, zum Ritus gehören kann.

Wenn man es für selbstverständlich hält, daß sich der Mensch an seiner Phantasie vergnügt, so bedenke man, daß diese Phantasie nicht wie ein gemaltes Bild oder ein plastisches Modell ist, sondern ein kompliziertes Gebilde aus heterogenen Bestandteilen: Wörtern und Bilder. Man wird dann das Operieren mit Schrift- und Lautzeichen nicht mehr in Gegensatz stellen zu dem Operieren mit 'Vorstellungsbildern' der Ereignisse.

Wir müssen die ganze Sprache durchpflugen.

After the description of any such magical cure we 'd like to add: If the illness doesn't understand *that*, then I don't know *how* one ought to say it.

I do not mean that it is especially *fire* that must make an impression on anyone. Fire no more than any other phenomenon, and one will impress this person and another that. For no phenomenon is particularly mysterious in itself, but any of them can become so to us, and it is precisely the characteristic feature of the awakening human spirit that a phenomenon has meaning for it. We could almost say, man is a ceremonious animal. This is partly false, partly nonsensical, but there is also something in it.

In other words, one might begin a book on anthropology in this way : When we watch the life and behaviour of men all over the earth we see that apart from what we might call animal activities, taking food &c., &c., men also carry out actions that bear a peculiar character and might be called ritualistic.

But then it is nonsense if we go on to say that the characteristic feature of *these* actions is that they spring from wrong ideas about the physics of things. (This is what Frazer does when he says magic is really false physics, or as the case may be, false medicine, technology, &c.)

What makes the character of ritual action is not any view or opinion, either right or wrong, although an opinion —a belief—itself can be ritualistic, or belong to a rite.

If we hold it a truism that people take pleasure in imagination, we should remember that this imagination is not like a painted picture or a three-dimensional model, but a complicated structure of heterogeneous elements : words and pictures. We shall then not think of operating with written or oral signs as something to be contrasted with the operation with " mental images " of the events.

We must plough over the whole of language.

Frazer : "... That these observances are dictated by fear of the ghost of the slain seems certain. ..." (S.212)   Aber warum gebraucht Frazer denn das Wort *ghost* ? Er versteht also sehr wohl diesen Aberglauben, da er ihn uns mit einem ihm geläufigen abergläubischen Wort erklärt. Oder vielmehr, er hätte daraus sehen können, daß auch in uns etwas für jene Handlungs- weisen der Wilden spricht. – Wenn ich, der ich nicht glaube, daß es irgendwo menschlich-übermenschliche Wesen gibt, die man Götter nen- nen kann – wenn ich sage: ,,ich fürchte die Rache der Götter", so zeigt das, daß ich damit etwas meinen kann, oder einer Empfindung Ausdruck geben kann, die nicht notwendig mit jenem Glauben verbunden ist.

Frazer wäre im Stande zu glauben, daß ein Wilder aus Irrtum stirbt. In den Volksschullesebüchern steht, daß Attila seine großen Kriegszüge unternommen hat, weil er glaubte, das Schwert des Donnergottes zu besitzen.

Frazer ist viel mehr savage, als die meisten seiner savages, denn diese werden nicht so weit vom Verständnis einer geistigen Angelegenheit entfernt sein, wie ein Engländer des 20sten Jahrhunderts. *Seine* Erklä- rungen der primitiven Gebräuche sind viel roher, als der Sinn dieser Gebräuche selbst.

Die historische Erklärung, die Erklärung als eine Hypothese der Ent- wicklung ist nur *eine* Art der Zusammenfassung der Daten – ihrer Synopsis. Es ist ebensowohl möglich, die Daten in ihrer Beziehung zu einander zu sehen und in ein allgemeines Bild zusammenzufassen, ohne es in Form einer Hypothese über die zeitliche Entwicklung zu machen.

Identifizierung der eigenen Götter mit Göttern andrer Völker. Man überzeugt sich davon, daß die Namen die gleiche Bedeutung haben.

"Und so deutet das Chor auf ein geheimes Gesetz" möchte man zu der Frazer'schen Tatsachensammlung sagen. Dieses Gesetz, diese Idee, *kann* ich nun durch eine Entwicklungshypothese darstellen oder auch, analog dem Schema einer Pflanze, durch das Schema einer religiösen Zeremonie,

Frazer : " ... That these observances are dictated by fear of the ghost of the slain seems certain. ... "(p.212)   But why does Frazer use the word " ghost " ?   He evidently understands this superstition well enough, since he uses a familiar superstitious word to describe it. Or rather, he might have seen from this that there is something in us too that speaks in support of those observances by the savages. — If I, who do not believe that somewhere or other there are human-superhuman beings which we might call gods—if I say " I fear the wrath of the gods," then this shows that with these words I can mean something or express a feeling that need not be connected with that belief.

Frazer might just as well believe that when a savage dies he is in error. In primary-school reading books it says that Attila undertook his great campaigns because he believed he possessed the sword of the god of thunder.

Frazer is much more savage than most of his savages, for these savages will not be so far from any understanding of spiritual matters as an Englishman of the twentieth century.   His explanations of the primitive observances are much cruder than the sense of the observances themselves.

An historical explanation, an explanation as an hypothesis of the development, is only *one* kind of summary of the data—of their synopsis. We can equally well see the data in their relations to one another and make a summary of them in a general picture without putting it in the form of an hypothesis regarding the temporal development.

Identifying one's own gods with the gods of other peoples.   One becomes convinced that the names have the same meaning.

"And all this points to some unknown law " is what we want to say about the material Frazer has collected.   I *can* set out this law in an hypothesis of development,* or again, in analogy with the schema of a plant I can give it in the schema of a religious ceremony, but I can also do it just by arranging the factual material so that we can easily pass from

* ?or evolution

oder aber durch die Gruppierung des Tatsachenmaterials allein, in einer *'übersichtlichen'* Darstellung.

Der Begriff der übersichtlichen Darstellung ist für uns von grundlegender Bedeutung. Er bezeichnet unsere Darstellungsform, die Art wie wir die Dinge sehen. (Eine Art der 'Weltanschauung' wie sie scheinbar für unsere Zeit typisch ist. Spengler.)

Diese übersichtliche Darstellung vermittelt das Verständnis, welches eben darin besteht, daß wir die "Zusammenhänge sehen". Daher die Wichtigkeit des Findens von *Zwischengliedern*.

Ein hypothetisches Zwischenglied aber soll in diesem Falle nichts tun, als die Aufmerksamkeit auf die Ähnlichkeit, den Zusammenhang, der *Tatsachen* lenken. Wie man eine interne Beziehung der Kreisform zur Ellipse dadurch illustrierte, daß man eine Ellipse allmählich in einen Kreis überführt; *aber nicht um zu behaupten, daß eine gewiße Ellipse tatsächlich, historisch, aus einem Kreis entstanden wäre* (Entwicklungshypothese), sondern nur um unser Auge für einen formalen Zusammenhang zu schärfen.

Aber auch die Entwicklungshypothese kann ich als weiter nichts sehen, als eine Einkleidung eines formalen Zusammenhangs.

one part to another and have a clear view of it—showing it in a " *perspicuous* " way.

For us the conception of a perspicuous presentation [a way of setting out the whole field together by making easy the passage from one part of it to another*] is fundamental. It indicates the form in which we write of things, the way in which we see things. (A kind of " *Weltanschauung* " that seems to be typical of our time. Spengler.)

This perspicuous presentation makes possible that understanding which consists just in the fact that we " see the connections ". Hence the importance of finding *intermediate links*.

But in our case an hypothetical link is not meant to do anything ex - cept draw attention to the similarity, the connection, between the *facts*. As one might illustrate the internal relation of a circle to an ellipse by gradually transforming an ellipse into a circle; *but not in order to assert that a given ellipse in fact, historically, came from a circle* (hypothesis of development†) but only to sharpen our eye for a formal connection.

But equally I might see the hypothesis of development as nothing but a way of expressing a formal connection.

---

* Introduced in translation, not in Wittgenstein's text. His word is " über-sichtlich". He uses this constantly in writing of logical notation and of mathematical proof, and it is clear what he means. So we ought to have an English word. We have put " perspicuous " here, but no-one uses this in English either. Perhaps a reader with more flexible wrists will hit on some-thing.

† ?or evolution

[Die folgenden Bemerkungen stehen im Maschineskript nicht mit den obigen zusammen:]

Ich möchte sagen: nichts zeigt unsere Verwandtschaft mit jenen Wilden besser, als daß Frazer ein ihm und uns so geläufiges Wort wie 'ghost' oder 'shade' bei der Hand hat, um die Ansichten dieser Leute zu beschreiben.

(Das ist ja doch etwas anderes, als wenn er etwa beschriebe, die Wilden bilden sich ein, daß ihnen ihr Kopf herunter fällt, wenn sie einen Feind erschlagen haben. Hier hätte *unsere Beschreibung* nichts Abergläubisches oder Magisches an sich.)

Ja, diese Sonderbarkeit bezieht sich nicht nur auf die Ausdrücke 'ghost' und 'shade', und es wird viel zu wenig Aufhebens davon gemacht, daß wir das Wort 'Seele', 'Geist' ('spirit') zu unserem eigenen gebildeten Vokabular zahlen. Dagegen ist es eine Kleinigkeit, daß wir nicht glauben, daß unsere Seele ißt und trinkt.

In unserer Sprache ist eine ganze Mythologie niedergelegt.

Austreiben des Todes oder Umbringen des Todes; aber anderseits wird er als Gerippe dargestellt, als selbst in gewissem Sinne tot. "As dead as death." "Nichts ist so tot wie der Tod; nichts ist so schön wie die Schönheit selbst." Das Bild, worunter man sich hier die Realität denkt ist, daß die Schönheit, der Tod, etc. die reinen (konzentrierten) Substanzen sind, während sie in einem schönen Gegenstand als Beimischung vorhanden sind. – Und erkenne ich hier nicht meine eigenen Betrachtungen über 'Gegenstand' und 'Komplex'? *

In den alten Riten haben wir den Gebrauch einer äußerst ausgebildeten Gebärdensprache.

Und wenn ich in Frazer lese, so möchte ich auf Schritt und Tritt sagen: Alle diese Prozesse, diese Wandlungen der Bedeutung, haben wir noch in unserer Wortsprache vor uns. Wenn das, was sich in der letzten Garbe verbirgt, der 'Kornwolf' genannt wird, aber auch diese Garbe selbst,

[The remarks up to this point form the " selection " Wittgenstein had typed as though forming a separate essay. The passages which follow now were not included in this, although they come—at various points— in the same large manuscript and in the revision and typing of it.]

I wish to say: nothing shows our kinship to those savages better than the fact that Frazer has at hand a word as familiar to us as " ghost " or " shade " to describe the way these people look at things.

(For this is something different from what it would be if he described, say, how savages imagine that their heads fall when they have slain an enemy ; where our *description* would have nothing superstitious or magical about it.)

What is queer in this is not limited to the expressions " ghost " and " shade ", and too little is made of the fact that we include the words " soul " and " spirit " in our own civilized vocabulary.   Compared with this, the fact that we do not believe our soul eats and drinks is a minor detail.

A whole mythology is deposited in our language.

To cast out death or to slay death; but he is also represented as a skeleton, as in some sense dead himself.   "As dead as death ".   " Nothing is so dead as death ; nothing is so beautiful as beauty itself." Here the image which we use in thinking of reality is that beauty, death &c. are the pure (concentrated) substances, and that they are found in the beautiful object as added ingredients of the mixture.—And do I not recognize here my own observations on " object " and " complex " ? *

What we have in the ancient rites is the practice of a highly cultivated gesture-language.

And when I read Frazer I keep wanting to say: All these processes, these changes of meaning, —we have them here still in our word-language. If what they call the " Corn-wolf " is what is hidden in the last sheaf; but also the last sheaf itself and also the man who binds it, we

* In *Tractatus Logico-Philosophicus* (*Logisch-Philosophische Abhandlung*), first published 1921.

und auch der Mann der sie bindet, so erkennen wir hierin einen uns wohl-
bekannten sprachlichen Vorgang. *

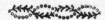

Ich könnte mir denken, daß ich die Wahl gehabt hätte, ein Wesen der
Erde als die Wohnung für meine Seele zu wählen, und daß mein Geist
dieses unansehnliche Geschöpf als seinen Sitz und Aussichtspunkt gewählt hätte. Etwa, weil ihm die Ausnahme eines schönen Sitzes zuwider
wäre. Dazu müsste freilich der Geist seiner selbst sehr sicher sein.

Man könnte sagen "jeder Aussicht ist ein Reiz abzugewinnen", aber das
wäre falsch. Richtig ist, zu sagen, jede Aussicht ist bedeutsam für den,
der sie bedeutsam sieht (das heißt aber nicht, sie anders sieht als sie ist).
Ja, in diesem Sinne ist jede Aussicht gleich bedeutsam.

Ja, es ist wichtig, daß ich auch die Verachtung jedes Andern für mich mir
zu eigen machen muß, als einen wesentlichen und bedeutsamen Teil der
Welt von meinem Ort gesehen.

Wenn es einem Menschen freigestellt wäre, sich in einen Baum eines
Waldes gebären zu lassen: so gäbe es Solche, die sich den schönsten oder
höchsten Baum aussuchen würden, solche die sich den kleinsten wählten
und solche die sich einen Durchschnitts- oder minderen Durchschnitts-
baum wählen würden, und zwar meine ich nicht aus **Philistrosität,**
sondern aus eben dem Grund, oder der Art von Grund, warum der Andre
den höchsten gewählt hat. Daß das Gefühl, welches wir für unser Leben
haben, mit dem eines solchen Wesens, das sich seinen Standpunkt in der
Welt wählen konnte, vergleichbar ist, liegt, glaube ich, dem Mythus –
oder dem Glauben – zu Grunde, wir hätten uns unsern Körper vor der
Geburt gewählt.

recognize in this a movement of language with which we are perfectly familiar.*

I could imagine that I had had to choose some being on earth as my soul's dwelling place, and that my spirit had chosen this insignificant creature as its seat and point from which it has to view things. Perhaps because a beautiful dwelling would be an exception and this repelled him.   Certainly the spirit would need to be very sure of itself to do this.

We might say " every view has its charm," but this would be wrong. What is true is that every view is significant for him who sees it so (but that does not mean " sees it as something other than it is ").   And in this sense every view is equally significant.

It is important also that the contempt each person feels for me is something I must make my own,   an essential and significant part of the world seen from the place where I am.

If a human being could choose to be born as a tree in a forest, then there would be some who would seek out the most beautiful or the highest tree for themselves, some who would choose the smallest and some who would choose an average or below-average tree, and I do not mean out of philistinism, but for just the reason, or the kind of reason, for which the other man chose the highest.   That the feeling we have for our life is comparable to that of a being who could choose his own standpoint in the world, is, I believe, the basis of the myth—or belief—that we choose our body before birth.

* " In various parts of Mecklenburg, where the belief in the Corn-wolf is particularly prevalent, everyone fears to cut the last corn, because they say the Wolf is sitting in it; ... the last bunch of corn is itself commonly called the Wolf, and the man who reaps it ... is himself called Wolf ... ." (*The Golden Bough*, p. 449)

Ich glaube, das Charakteristische des primitiven Menschen ist es, daß er nicht aus *Meinungen* handelt (dagegen Frazer).

Ich lese, unter vielen ähnlichen Beispielen, von einem Regenkönig in Afrika, zu dem die Leute um Regen bitten *wenn die Regenperiode kommt.** Aber das heißt doch, daß sie nicht eigentlich meinen, er könne Regen machen, sonst würden sie es in den trockenen Perioden des Jahres, in der das Land "a parched and arid desert" ist, machen. Denn wenn man annimmt, daß die Leute einmal aus Dummheit dieses Amt des Regenkönigs eingesetzt haben, so ist es doch gewiß klar, daß sie schon vorher die Erfahrung hatten, daß im März der Regen beginnt und sie hätten dann den Regenkönig für den übrigen Teil des Jahres funktionieren lassen. Oder auch so: Gegen morgen, wenn die Sonne aufgehen will, werden von den Menschen Riten des Tagwerdens zelebriert aber nicht in der Nacht, sondern da brennen sie einfach Lampen.

---

* " ... the Kings of the Rain, *Mata Kodou*, who are credited with the power of giving rain at the proper time, that is, in the rainy season. Before the rains begin to fall at the end of March the country is a parched and arid desert; and the cattle, which form the people's chief wealth, perish for lack

The characteristic feature of primitive man, I believe, is that he does not act from *opinions* he holds about things (as Frazer thinks).

I read, amongst many similar examples, of a rain-king in Africa to whom the people appeal for rain *when the rainy season comes.*＊   But surely this means that they do not actually think he can make rain, otherwise they would do it in the dry periods in which the land is " a parched and arid desert ".   For if we do assume that it was stupidity that once led the people to institute this office of Rain King, still they obviously knew from experience that the rains begin in March, and it would have been the Rain King's duty to perform in other periods of the year.   Or again : towards morning, when the sun is about to rise, people celebrate rites of the coming of day, but not at night, for then they simply burn lamps.

of grass. So, when the end of March draws on, each householder betakes himself to the King of Rain and offers him a cow that he may make the blessed waters of heaven drip on the brown and withered pastures." (*The Golden Bough*, p. 107)

II

So einfach es klingt: der Unterschied zwischen Magie und Wissenschaft kann dahin ausgedrückt werden, daß es in der Wissenschaft einen Fortschritt gibt, aber nicht in der Magie. Die Magie hat keine Richtung der Entwicklung, die in ihr selbst liegt.

S. 617 ff.   (In Chapter LXII: The Fire Festivals of Europe.)
Das Auffallendste scheint mir außer den Ähnlichkeiten die Verschiedenheit aller diesen Riten zu sein. Es ist eine Mannigfaltigkeit von Gesichtern mit gemeinsamen Zügen, die da und dort immer wieder auftauchen. Und was man tun möchte ist, Linien ziehen, die die gemeinsamen Bestandteile verbinden. Es fehlt dann noch ein Teil der Betrachtung und es ist der, welcher dieses Bild mit unsern eigenen Gefühlen und Gedanken in Verbindung bringt. Dieser Teil gibt der Betrachtung ihre Tiefe.

In allen diesen Gebräuchen sieht man allerdings etwas, der Ideen-assoziation ähnliches und mit ihr verwandtes. Man könnte von einer Assoziation der Gebräuche reden.

So soon as any sparks were emitted by means of the violent friction, they applied a species of agaric which grows on old birch-trees, and is very combustible.   This fire had the appearance of being immediately derived from heaven, and manifold were the virtues ascribed to it.

(*The Golden Bough*, S. 618)

Nichts spricht dafür, warum das Feuer mit solchem Nimbus umgeben sein sollte. Und, wie seltsam, was heißt es eigentlich, "es schien vom Himmel gekommen zu sein"? von welchem Himmel? Nein es ist gar nicht selbstverständlich, daß das Feuer so betrachtet wird – aber es wird eben so betrachtet.

II

Simple though it may sound, we can express the difference between
science and magic if we say that in science there is progress, but not in
magic. There is nothing in magic to show the direction of any development.

Page 617ff. (in Chapter LXII, " The Fire Festivals Of Europe ")
The most noticeable thing seems to me not merely the similarities
but also the differences throughout all these rites. It is a wide variety of
faces with common features that keep showing in one place and in
another. And one would like to draw lines joining the parts that various
faces have in common. But then a part of our contemplation would
still be lacking, namely what connects this picture with our own feelings
and thoughts. This part gives the contemplation its depth.

In all these practices we see something that is similar, at any rate, to the
association of ideas and related to it. We could speak of an association
of practices.

So soon as any sparks were emitted by means of the violent friction,
they applied a species of agaric which grows on old birch-trees, and is
very combustible. This fire had the appearance of being immediately
derived from heaven, and manifold were the virtues ascribed to it.
                              (*The Golden Bough*, p. 618)

There is nothing to explain why the fire should have such a nimbus sur-
rounding it. And what a queer thing, what does it actually mean, " it
had the appearance of being derived from heaven " ? From what
heaven ? No, it by no means goes without saying, that the fire is regarded in this way—but that is how it is regarded.

The person who officiated as master of the feast produced a large cake
baked with eggs and scalloped round the edge, called *am bonnach beal-
tine*—i.e., the Beltane cake. It was divided into a number of pieces,
and distributed in great form to the company. There was one particular
piece which whoever got was called *cailleach beal-tine*—i.e., the Beltane *carline*, a term of great reproach. Upon his being known, part of
the company laid hold of him and made a show of putting him into the
fire.... And while the feast was fresh in people's memory, they affected
to speak of the *cailleach beal-tine* as dead. (S. 618)

Hier scheint die Hypothese erst der Sache Tiefe zu geben. Und man kann
sich an die Erklärung des seltsamen Verhältnisses von Siegfried und
Brunhild in unsrem Nibelungenlied erinnern. Nämlich, daß Siegfried
Brunhilde schon früher einmal gesehen zu haben scheint. Es ist nun klar,
daß, was diesem Gebrauch Tiefe gibt, sein *Zusammenhang* mit dem
Verbrennen eines Menschen ist. Wenn es bei irgendeinem Fest Sitte wäre,
daß Menschen (wie beim Roß-und-Reiter-Spiel) auf einander reiten, so
würden wir darin nichts sehen als eine Form des Tragens, die an das
Reiten des Menschen auf einem Pferd erinnert; – wüßten wir aber, daß
es unter vielen Völkern Sitte gewesen wäre, etwa Sklaven als Reittiere zu
benützen, und so beritten gewisse Feste zu feiern, so würden wir jetzt in
dem harmlosen Gebrauch unserer Zeit etwas Tieferes und weniger
Harmloses sehen. Die Frage ist: haftet dieses – sagen wir – Finstere dem
Gebrauch des Beltane Feuers, wie er vor 100 Jahren geübt wurde, an
sich an, oder nur dann, wenn die Hypothese seiner Entstehung sich
bewahrheiten sollte. Ich glaube es ist offenbar die innere Natur des neu-
zeitlichen Gebrauchs selbst, die uns finster anmutet, und die uns bekannten Tatsachen von Menschenopfern weisen nur die Richtung in der wir
den Gebrauch ansehen sollen. Wenn ich von der inneren Natur des
Gebrauchs rede, meine ich alle Umstände, in denen er geübt wird und
die in dem Bericht von so einem Fest nicht enthalten sind, da sie nicht
sowohl in bestimmten Handlungen bestehen, die das Fest charakterisie-
ren, als in dem was man den Geist des Festes nennen könnte, welcher
beschrieben würde indem man z.B. die Art von Leuten beschriebe, die
daran teilnehmen, ihre übrige Handlungsweise, d.h. ihren Charakter, die
Art der Spiele, die sie sonst spielen. Und man würde dann sehen, daß das
Finstere im Charakter dieser Menschen selbst liegt.

The person who officiated as master of the feast produced a large cake baked with eggs and scalloped round the edge, called *am bonnach beal-tine*—i.e., the Beltane cake. It was divided into a number of pieces, and distributed in great form to the company. There was one particular piece which whoever got was called *cailleach beal-tine*—i.e., the Beltane *carline*, a term of great reproach. Upon his being known, part of the company laid hold of him and made a show of putting him into the fire .... And while the feast was fresh in people's memory, they affected to speak of the *cailleach beal-tine* as dead. (p.618)

Here it seems as though it were the hypothesis that gives the matter depth.   And we may remember the explanation of the strange relationship between Siegfried and Brunhilde in our *Niebelungenlied*.   Namely that Siegfried seems to have seen Brunhilde before. It is clear that what gives this practice depth is its *connection* with the burning of a man. If it were the custom at some festival for men to ride on one another (as in horse-and-rider games), we would see nothing more in this than a way of carrying someone which reminds us of men riding horses.   But if we knew that among many peoples it had been the custom, say, to use slaves as mounts and to celebrate certain festivals mounted in this way, we should then see in the harmless practice of our time something deeper and less harmless.   The question is: is what we may call the sinister character of the Beltane fire festival as it was practised a hundred years ago—is this a character of the practice in itself, or only if the hypothesis regarding its origin is confirmed? I think it is clear that what gives us a sinister impression is the inner nature of the practice as performed in recent times, and the facts of human sacrifice as we know them only indicate the direction in which we ought to see it.   When I speak of the inner nature of the practice I mean all those circumstances in which it is carried out that are not included in the account of the festival, because they consist not so much in particular actions which characterize it, but rather in what we might call the spirit of the festival: which would be described by, for example, describing the sort of people that take part, their way of behaviour at other times, i.e. their character, and the other kinds of games that they play.   And we should then see that what is sinister lies in the character of these people themselves.

In ... western Perthshire, the Beltane custom was still in vogue towards the end of the eighteenth century. It has been described as follows by the parish minister of the time : " ... They put all the bits of the cake into a bonnet. Every one, blindfold, draws out a portion. ... Whoever draws the black bit is the *devoted* person who is to be sacrificed to *Baal* ... ."

Thomas Pennant, who travelled in Perthshire in the year 1769, tells us that " ... every one takes a cake of oatmeal, upon which are raised nine square knobs, each dedicated to some particular being.... "

Another writer of the eighteenth century has described the Beltane festival as it was held in the parish of Logierait in Perthshire. He says : " ... These dishes they eat with a sort of cakes baked for the occasion, and having small lumps in the form of *nipples*, raised all over the surface." ... We may conjecture that the cake with knobs was formerly used for the purpose of determining who should be the "Beltane carline" or victim doomed to the flames. (S.618, 619)

Hier sieht etwas aus wie die Überreste eines Losens. Und durch diesen Aspekt gewinnt es plötzlich Tiefe. Würden wir erfahren, daß der Kuchen mit den Knöpfen in einem bestimmten Fall etwa ursprünglich zu Ehren eines Knopfmachers zu seinem Geburtstag gebacken worden sei, und sich der Gebrauch dann in der Gegend erhalten habe, so würde dieser Gebrauch tatsächlich alles 'Tiefe' verlieren, es sei denn daß es in seiner gegenwärtigen Form an sich liegt. Aber man sagt in so einem Fall oft: "dieser Gebrauch ist offenbar uralt". Woher weiß man das? Ist es nur, weil man historisches Zeugnis über derartige alte Gebräuche hat? Oder hat es noch einen andern Grund, einen, den man durch Interpretation gewinnt? Aber auch wenn die vorzeitliche Herkunft des Gebrauchs und die Abstammung von einem früheren Gebrauch historisch erwiesen ist, so ist es doch möglich, daß der Gebrauch heute *gar nichts* mehr finsteres an sich hat, daß nichts von dem vorzeitlichen Grauen an ihm hangen geblieben ist. Vielleicht wird er heute nur mehr von Kindern geübt, die im Kuchenbacken und Verzieren mit Knopfen wetteifern. Dann liegt das Tiefe also nur im Gedanken an jene Abstammung. Aber diese kann doch ganz unsicher sein und man möchte sagen: "Wozu sich über eine so unsichere Sache sorgen" (wie eine rückwärts schauende Kluge Else). Aber solche Sorgen sind es nicht. – Vor allem: woher die Sicherheit, daß ein solcher Gebrauch uralt sein muß (was sind unsere Daten, was ist die Verifikation)? Aber haben wir denn eine Sicherheit, können wir uns nicht darin irren und des Irrtums historisch überführt werden? Gewiß, aber

In ... western Perthshire, the Beltane custom was still in vogue towards the end of the eighteenth century. It has been described as follows by the parish minister of the time : " ... They put all the bits of the cake into a bonnet. Every one, blindfold, draws out a portion. ... Whoever draws the black bit is the *devoted* person who is to be sacrificed to *Baal* ... ."

Thomas Pennant, who travelled in Perthshire in the year 1769, tells us that " ... every one takes a cake of oatmeal, upon which are raised nine square knobs, each dedicated to some particular being... ."

Another writer of the eighteenth century has described the Beltane festival as it was held in the parish of Logierait in Perthshire. He says : " ... These dishes they eat with a sort of cakes baked for the occasion, and having small lumps in the form of *nipples*, raised all over the surface." ... We may conjecture that the cake with knobs was formerly used for the purpose of determining who should be the " Beltane carline " or victim doomed to the flames. (pp. 618, 619)

Here something looks like the ruins of a casting of lots.   And through this aspect it suddenly gains depth.   Should we learn that the cake with the knobs in a particular case had originally been baked, say, in honour of a button-maker on his birthday and the practice had then persisted in the district, it would in fact lose all " depth ", unless this should lie in the present form of the practice itself.

But in a case like this we often say: " this practice is obviously age-old."   How do we know that ?   Is it only because we have historical evidence regarding ancient practices of this sort ?   Or is there another reason, one that comes through interpretation ?   But even if its ancient origin and its descent from an earlier practice is established by history, it is still possible that there is nothing sinister at all about the practice today, that no trace of the ancient horror is left on it.   Perhaps it is only performed by children now, who have contests in baking cakes and decorating them with knobs.   So that the depth lies solely in the thought of that ancestry.   Yet this ancestry may be very uncertain and one feels like saying : " Why make what is so uncertain into something to worry about ? " (like a backwards-looking Kluge Else).   But worries of that kind are not involved here.

Above all : whence the certainty that a practice of this kind must be age-old (what are the data, what is the verification) ?   But *have* we any certainty, may we not have been led into a mistake because we were over-impressed by historical considerations ?   Certainly, but that still

es bleibt dann noch immer etwas, dessen wir sicher sind. Wir würden dann sagen: "Gut, in diesem Fall mag die Herkunft anders sein, aber im allgemeinen ist sie sicher die Vorzeitliche." Was uns dafür *Evidenz* ist, das muß die Tiefe dieser Annahme enthalten. Und diese Evidenz ist wieder eine nicht-hypothetische, psychologische. Wenn ich nämlich sage: das Tiefe in diesem Gebrauch liegt in seiner Herkunft *wenn* sie sich so zugetragen hat. So liegt also entweder das Tiefe in dem Gedanken an so eine Herkunft, oder das Tiefe ist selbst hypothetisch und man kann nur sagen: *Wenn* es sich so zugetragen hat, so war das eine finstere tiefe Geschichte. Ich will sagen: Das Finstere, Tiefe liegt nicht darin, daß es sich mit der Geschichte dieses Gebrauchs so verhalten hat, denn vielleicht hat es sich gar nicht so verhalten; auch nicht darin, daß es sich vielleicht oder wahrscheinlich so verhalten hat, sondern in dem, was mir Grund gibt, das anzunehmen. Ja, woher überhaupt das Tiefe und Finstere im Menschenopfer? Denn sind es nur die Leiden des Opfers, die uns den Eindruck machen? Krankheiten aller Art, die mit ebensoviel Leiden verbunden sind, rufen diesen Eindruck *doch* nicht hervor. Nein, dies Tiefe und Finstere versteht sich nicht von selbst wenn wir nur die Geschichte der äußeren Handlung erfahren, sondern *wir* tragen es wieder hinein aus einer Erfahrung in unserm Innern.

Die Tatsache, daß das Los durch einen Kuchen gezogen wird, hat auch etwas besonders schreckliches (beinahe wie der Verrat durch einen Kuß), und daß uns das besonders schrecklich anmutet, hat wieder eine wesentliche Bedeutung für die Untersuchung solcher Gebräuche.

Es ist, wenn ich so einen Gebrauch sehe, von ihm höre, wie wenn ich einen Mann sehe wie er bei geringfügigem Anlaß streng mit einem Andern spricht, und aus dem Ton der Stimme und dem Gesicht merke, daß dieser Mann bei gegebenem Anlaß furchtbar sein kann. Der Eindruck, den ich hier erhalte, kann ein sehr tiefer und außerordentlich ernster sein.

Die *Umgebung* einer Handlungsweise.

Eine Überzeugung liegt jedenfalls den Annahmen über den Ursprung des Beltanefestes – z.B. – zu Grunde; die ist, daß solche Feste nicht von einem Menschen, sozusagen aufs Geratewohl erfunden werden, sondern

leaves something of which we are sure. We would then say : " Very well, the origin in this case may be different, but as a general rule certainly it is age-old. " It is our *evidence* for it, that holds what is deep in this assumption. And this evidence is again non-hypothetical, psychological. For when I say : what is deep in this practice lies in its origin, if it *did* come about like that, then either the depth lies in the idea (the thought) of [its descent from] such an origin, or else the depth is itself **hypothetical and we can only say:** *if* **that is how it went, then it was a deep and sinister business. What I want to say is : What is sinister, deep, does not lie in the fact that that is how the history of this practice went, for perhaps it did not go that way; nor in the fact that perhaps or probably it was that, but in what it is that gives me reason to assume it.**

What makes human sacrifice something deep and sinister anyway ? Is it only the suffering of the victim that impresses us in this way ? All manner of diseases bring just as much suffering and do *not* make this impression. No, this deep and sinister aspect is not obvious just from learning the history of the external action, but *we* impute it from an experience in ourselves.

The fact that for the lots they use a cake has something especially terrible (almost like betrayal through a kiss), and that this does seem especially terrible to us is of central importance in our investigation of practices like these.

If I see such a practice, or hear of it, it is like seeing a man speaking sternly to another because of something quite trivial, and noticing in the tone of his voice and in his face that on occasion this man can be frightening. The impression I get from this may be a very deep and extremely serious one.

The *environment* of a way of acting.

There is one conviction that underlies [or is taken for granted in] the hypotheses about the origin of, say, the Beltane festival ; namely that festivals of this kind are not so to speak haphazard inventions of

eine unendlichviel breitere Basis brauchen, um sich zu erhalten. Wollte ich ein Fest erfinden, so würde es baldigst aussterben oder aber solcherweise modifiziert werden, daß es einem allgemeinen Hang der Leute entspricht.

Was aber wehrt sich dagegen anzunehmen, das Beltanefest sei immer in der gegenwärtigen (oder jüngstvergangenen) Form gefeiert worden? Man möchte sagen: Es ist zu sinnlos um so erfunden worden zu sein. Ist es nicht, wie wenn ich eine Ruine sehe und sage: das muß einmal ein Haus gewesen sein, denn niemand würde einen so beschaffenen Haufen behauener und unregelmäßiger Steine errichten? Und wenn gefragt würde: Woher weißt du das? so könnte ich nur sagen: meine Erfahrung mit den Menschen lehrt es mich. Ja, selbst da wo sie wirklich Ruine bauen, nehmen sie die Formen von eingestürzten Häusern her.

Man könnte auch so sagen: Wer uns mit der Erzählung vom Beltanefest einen Eindruck machen wollte, brauchte jedenfalls die Hypothese von seiner Herkunft nicht zu äußern, sondern er brauchte uns nur das Material (das zu dieser Hypothese führt) vorlegen und nichts weiter dazu sagen. Nun möchte man vielleicht sagen: "Freilich, weil der Hörer oder Leser den Schluß selber ziehen wird!" Aber muß er diesen Schluß explizite ziehen? also, überhaupt, ziehen? Und was ist es denn für ein Schluß? Daß das oder jenes *wahrscheinlich* ist?! Und wenn er den Schluß selber ziehen kann, wie soll ihm der Schluß einen Eindruck machen? was ihm den Eindruck macht muß doch das sein, was *er* nicht gemacht hat! Impressioniert ihn also erst die geäußerte Hypothese (ob von ihm oder andern geäußert), oder schon das Material zu ihr? Aber könnte ich da nicht ebensogut fragen: Wenn ich sehe wie Einer umgebracht wird, – impressioniert mich da einfach was ich sehe oder erst die Hypothese, daß hier ein Mensch umgebracht wird?

Aber es ist ja nicht einfach der Gedanke an die mögliche Herkunft des Beltanefestes welche den Eindruck mit sich führt sondern, was man die ungeheure Wahrscheinlichkeit dieses Gedankens nennt. Als das was vom Material hergenommen ist.

So wie das Beltanefest auf uns gekommen ist, ist es ja ein Schauspiel und ähnlich wie wenn Kinder Räuber spielen. Aber doch nicht so. Denn

one man but need an infinitely broader basis if they are to persist.   If
I tried to invent a festival it would very soon die out or else be so modi-
fied that it corresponded to a general inclination in people.

But what makes us unwilling to assume that the Beltane festival has
always been celebrated in its present (or very recent) form ?   We feel
like saying : it is too meaningless to have been invented in this form.
Isn't it like this when I see a ruin and say : that must have been a house
once, for nobody would have built up hewn and irregular stones into a
heap constructed like this one.   And if someone asked, how do you
know that ?   I could only say : it is what my experience of people
teaches me.   And even where people do really build ruins, they give
them the form of tumbled-down houses.

We might put it this way : Anyone who wanted to impress us with
the story of the Beltane festival would not need to explain the hypothesis
of its origin anyway ; he would only have to lay before us the material
(which leads him to this hypothesis) and say nothing more.   Here one
may be inclined to say : " Of course, because the listener or reader will
draw the conclusion himself ! "   But must he draw the conclusion ex-
plicitly ? i.e., draw it at all ?   And what sort of conclusion is it ?
That this or that is *probable* ?   And if he can draw the conclusion himself, how should the conclusion make an impression on him ?   What
makes the impression must surely be something *he* has not done.   Is it
only the hypothesis when expressed by him or by someone else that impresses him, or is he already impressed by the material for it ?   But
could I not just as well ask :   When I see someone being killed—is it
simply what I see that makes an impression on me or does this come
with the hypothesis that someone is being killed here ?
    But it is not just the idea of the possible origin of the Beltane festival
that makes it impressive, but what we call the overwhelming probability
of this idea.   What we get from the material.
    The Beltane festival as it has come down to us is the performance of
a play, something like children playing at robbers.   But then again it is
not like this.   For even though it is prearranged so that the side which
saves the victim wins, there is still the infusion of a mood or state of

wenn es auch abgekartet ist, daß die Partei die das Opfer rettet gewinnt, so hat doch, was geschieht, noch immer einen Temperamentszusatz, den die bloße schauspielerische Darstellung nicht hat. Aber auch wenn es sich bloß um eine ganz kühle Darstellung handelte, würden wir uns doch beunruhigt fragen: Was soll diese Darstellung, was ist ihr *Sinn*?! Und sie könnte uns abgesehen von jeder Deutung dann durch ihre eigentümliche Sinnlosigkeit beunruhigen. (Was zeigt, welcher Art der Grund so einer Beunruhigung sein kann.) Würde nun etwa eine harmlose Deutung gegeben: Das Los werde einfach geworfen, damit man das Vergnügen hätte, jemanden damit drohen zu können ins Feuer geworfen zu werden, was nicht angenehm sei; so wird das Beltanefest viel ähnlicher einem jener Belustigungen wo einer der Gesellschaft gewisse Grausamkeiten zu erdulden hat und die so wie sie sind ein Bedürfnis befriedigen. Und das Beltanefest würde durch so eine Erklärung auch jedes Geheimnisvolle verlieren, wenn es eben nicht selbst in der Handlung wie in der Stimmung von solchen gewöhnlichen Räuberspielen etc. abwiche.

Ebenso, daß Kinder an gewissen Tagen einen Strohmann verbrennen, auch wenn dafür keine Erklärung gegeben würde, könnte uns beunruhigen. Seltsam, daß *ein Mensch* festlich von ihnen verbrannt werden sollte! Ich will sagen: die Lösung ist nicht beunruhigender als das Rätsel.

Warum soll es aber nicht wirklich nur (oder doch zum Teil) der *Gedanke* sein, der mir den Eindruck gibt? Sind denn Vorstellungen nicht furchtbar? Kann mir bei dem Gedanken, daß der Kuchen mit den Knöpfen einmal dazu gedient hat das Todesopfer auszulosen, nicht schaurig zumut werden? Hat nicht der *Gedanke* etwas Furchtbares? – Ja, aber das was ich in jenen Erzählungen sehe gewinnen sie doch durch die Evidenz, auch durch solche, die damit nicht unmittelbar verbunden zu sein scheint, – durch den Gedanken an den Menschen und seine Vergangenheit, durch all das Seltsame, das ich in mir und in den Andern sehe, gesehen und gehört habe.

mind in what is happening which a theatrical production does not have. And even if it were a perfectly cool performance we should be uneasy and ask ourselves: What is this performance trying to do, what is its point ? And apart from any interpretation its queer pointlessness could make us uneasy. (Which shows the kind of reason that an uneasiness of this sort can have.) Suppose some harmless interpretation: perhaps that they cast lots just so that they can have the fun of threatening to throw someone in the fire, which would be disagreeable ; then the Beltane festival becomes much more like one of those practical jokes in which one of the company has to submit to cruel treatment and which satisfy a need just in this form. Such an explanation would take all mystery from the Beltane festival, were it not that the festival is something different in action and in mood from those familiar games of robbers &c.

In the same way, the fact that on certain days children burn a straw man could make us uneasy, even if no explanation [hypothesis] were given. Strange that they should celebrate by burning a *man* ! What I want to say is : the solution is not any more disquieting than the riddle.

But why should it not really be (partly, anyway) just the *idea* that makes the impression on me ? Aren't ideas frightening ? Can I not feel horror from the thought that the cake with the knobs once served to select by lot the victim to be sacrificed ? Hasn't the *thought* something terrible ? — Yes, but that which I see in those stories is something they acquire, after all, from the evidence, including such evidence as does not seem directly connected with them—from the thought of man and his past, from the strangeness of what I see in myself and in others, what I have seen and have heard.